This igloo book belongs to:

....

igloobooks

Published in 2020
by Igloo Books Ltd
Cottage Farm
Sywell
NN6 0BJ
www.igloobooks.com

0120 003
4 6 8 10 11 9 7 5 3
ISBN 978-1-78905-658-7

Written by Melanie Joyce
Illustrated by Ben Whitehouse

Cover designed by Lee Italiano
Interiors designed by Amy Bradford
Edited by Hannah Cather

Printed and manufactured in China

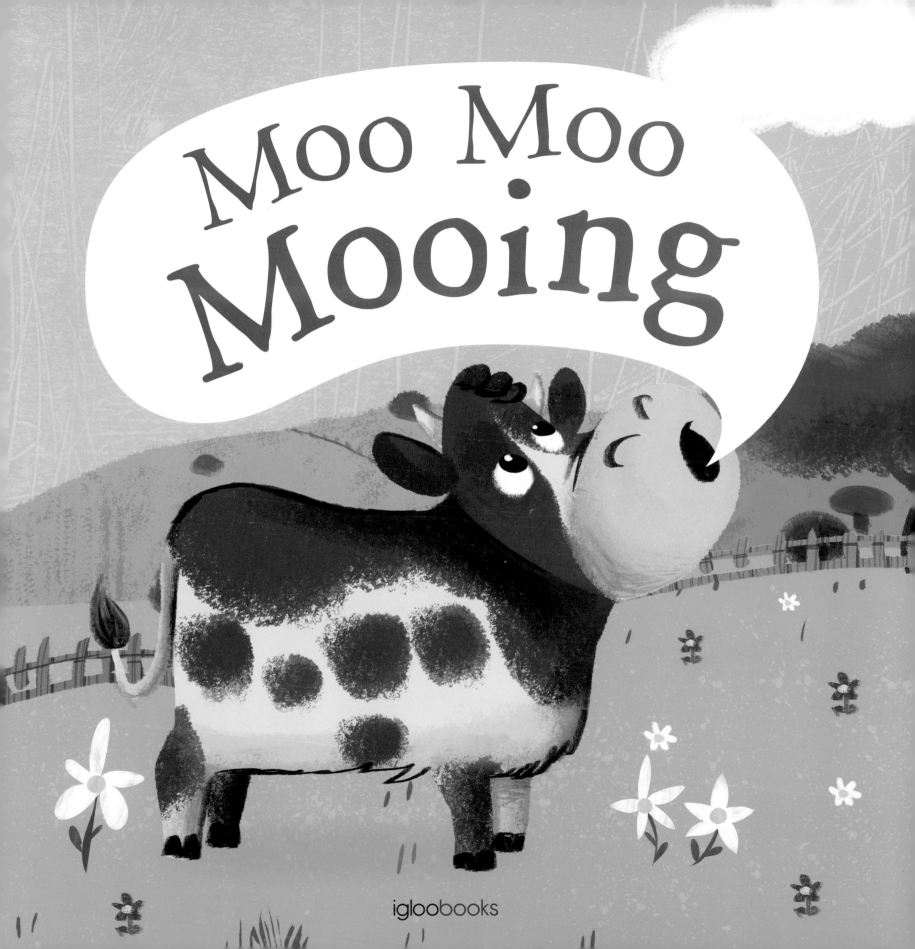

Moo Moo Mooing

igloobooks

The cows in the meadow are **moo-moo-mooing**, chomping on the green grass, **chew-chew-chewing**.

Moo goes one cow and moo goes another.
Moo-moo-moo go all the cows together.

Moo!

Moo-moo-chew on the noisy little farm.

Oink-oink-oink go the pigs in the sty,
snuffling in the mud as the tractor chugs by.

Moo!

Here comes the swill with a **sploosh-sploosh-Splosh.**
Chomp-Slurp-chomp go the pigs in the trough.

Oink-splosh-Slurp on the noisy little farm.

The ducks in the pond are...

... quack-quack-quacking,

nestling in the nest where the eggs are **cracking**.

A crick... a **crack**... then, tiny little wings.
Peep-peep-**peep** go the new ducklings.

Moo!

Quack-crack-peep on the noisy little farm.

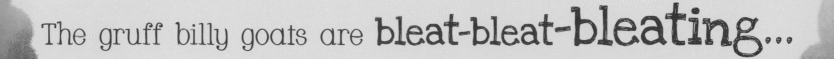

The gruff billy goats are **bleat-bleat-bleating...**

... **crunching** all the cabbages, **eat-eat-eating.**

Greedy goats love to **crunch** and **munch.**

Moo!

They have even eaten Farmer Ben's lunch!

Bleat-crunch-munch on the noisy little farm.

The broody hens are

scratch-scratch-scratching...

... clucking at the cute chicks hatch-hatch-hatching.

Farmer Ben's truck is **toot-toot-tooting...**

Moo!

... driving to the paddock and **hoot-hoot-hooting.**

He's got apples and carrots and nice fresh [...]

Clip-clop go the horses as they **neigh-neigh-n[...]**

Toot-hoot-neigh on the noisy little farm.

Vrmm-vrmm-Vrmm

goes Farmer Ben's truck.

In the meadow, the sheep are stuck.

The kittens in the kitchen are **lap-lap-lapping.**

The puppies in the basket are **yap-yap-yapping.**

Woof-woof-meow, they chase and play.

It's very noisy in the farmhouse today.

Lap-yap-meow on the noisy little farm.

The golden sun is sink-sink-sinking.

All the little stars are happily twinkling.

Moo!

Evening shadows
come slowly **creeping**.

Soon, all the animals will be **sleeping**.
Creep-creep-Sleep on the noisy little farm.

The cows in the field stop **mooing** and **chewing.**

There's no more **clucking** or **munching** or **scratching.**
No more **quacking, cracking, oinking** or **bleating.**

No more splooshing, slurping, tooting, hooting, scratching, hatching, yapping or lapping.

Zzzz-zzzz-ZZZZ.

Everyone's asleep on the quiet little farm.